# Written Anything Good Lately?

## By Susan Allen and Jane Lindaman
## Illustrated by Vicky Enright

M Millbrook Press/Minneapolis

For my son Tim. "You're the Best."—Susan

This one is for my mom and all my dear aunts.—Jane

To Sean, Nicky, the "real" Mrs. Chapin, and West Elementary School. Thanks.—Vicky

Millbrook Press
A division of Lerner Publishing Group, Inc.
241 First Avenue North
Minneapolis, Minnesota 55401 USA

For reading levels and more information, look up this title at www.lernerbooks.com.

Library of Congress Cataloging-in-Publication Data
Allen, Susan, 1951-
Written anything good lately? / by Susan Allen and Jane Lindaman ; illustrated by Vicky Enright.
p. cm.
ISBN 978-0-7613-2426-3 (lib. bdg. : alk. paper)
ISBN 978-0-8225-6522-2 (EB pdf)
1. Rhetoric—Juvenile literature. I. Lindaman, Jane. II. Enright, Vicky, ill. III. Title.
P301.A445 2006          808—dc22          2005007633

Manufactured in the United States of America
6 - VP - 2/1/16

Written anything good lately?

I was born at 5 o'clock in the morning.

When I was four, I saw my first T-rex skeletons.

My brother was born on the first day of school.

Now I know how to write. I read what I write about dinosaurs to my brother.

# An autobiography

A brilliant book report

Read Anything
Good Lately?

Christmas and
Chanukah cards for my class

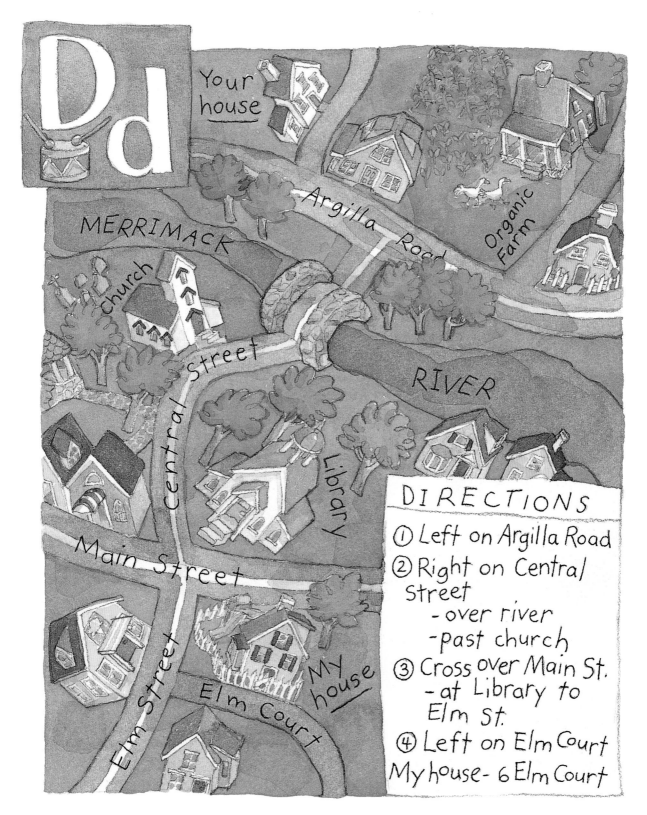

**DIRECTIONS**
① Left on Argilla Road
② Right on Central Street
 - over river
 - past church
③ Cross over Main St.
 - at Library to Elm St.
④ Left on Elm Court
My house - 6 Elm Court

Detailed directions for driving to my house

An essay for my English class

I think it is important to think about other people, and to help people any way we can. My mom and I and our dog visited a nursing home and we felt happy to know...

A **f**able about
a friendless fox

A greeting card for
my grandparents

A heavenly Haiku

Haiku
Huffing and puffing
Hiking high up on the hill
Halfway to heaven

An invitation to an
ice cream party

My feet touched
the bottom, so
I was not
scared. But
my Mom was
scared, and
she...

# A journal of my
# July vacation

Kudos (that means *compliments*) for kids in my class

A long letter to my pen pal in London

A myth about
magical monsters

A newsletter for
my nature club

An outline of
my observations

A play to perform
for our parents

The Story of Little
Red Riding Hood
and the Good Wolf

RRH: What big ears
you have!
Wolf: That's not very
nice.
RRH: What big teeth
you have!
Wolf: I know. I
brush and floss
every day.
RRH: What big feet...

Answering the questions on a **quiz**

Most rainforests are near the equator. Most rainforests have at least eighty inches of rain a year. About half the world's species of plants and animals →

A report on the rainforest

A sensational speech
for social studies class

A thank-you note
to my terrific teacher

A User ID for my
new computer

A valentine **v**erse
for my best friend

A word wall for
our classroom

X's and O's for my
"X-tra special" friend

*Dear Jill,*
*Happy birthday*
*to my very*
*best friend!*
*XXXXXo*
*XOOOOOX*
*love Sara*

Mrs. Chapin's class had a great year!

Here's one of our most golden memorable days, where friendship and learning really began.

A yearbook page for my class

Zigzags and zeros
until the next idea comes along....

What have you written lately?

# About the Authors and Artist

**Susan Allen** has been connecting children and books for the past thirty-five years as an elementary school teacher and librarian in Phoenix, Arizona. **Jane Lindaman** has been an elementary teacher in Phoenix and in Gilbert, Arizona. They wrote this book because they wanted children to understand that writing is a skill that is used in many different ways. And, without writers, what would we all have to read?

**Vicky Enright** has illustrated a number of highly successful Kathy Ross craft titles, including *Crafts for All Seasons*, and *The Storytime Craftbook*. Vicky lives in Andover, Massachusetts, with her husband and two children, and two huge Labrador retriever dogs.

Together Jane and Susan and Vicky created the companion volume to this book, *Read Anything Good Lately?*